The Seed and the Flower

By

Olaf Stapledon

British Library Cataloguing-in-Publication Data
A catalogue record for this book is available from the
British Library

Olaf Stapledon

William Olaf Stapledon was born on 10th May 1886 in Wallasey, on the Wirral Peninsula near Liverpool, in England. Stapledon attended Abbotsholme school before enrolling at Balloil College, Oxford, where he received a BA in Modern History in 1909, and then an MA in 1913.

Stapledon was a conscientious objector during the First World War and, instead of fighting, worked with the Friend's Ambulance Unit in France and Belgium between 1915 and 1919. Upon his return he completed a Ph.D. in philosophy at the University of Liverpool. His first work of prose *A Modern Theory of Ethics* (1929) was based on his doctoral thesis. The following year, Stapledon published his first work of fiction *Last and First Men* (1930), the success of which enabled him to become a full-time writer.

Stapledon had a great impact in the field of science fiction, influencing notable authors such as Arthur C. Clarke and Brian Aldiss. His novel *Starmaker* (1937) also inspired physicist Freeman Dyson to come up with the concept for what are now known as 'Dyson Spheres', a method of obtaining vast amounts of energy from a star.

The Seed and the Flower

(1916)

God sowed a seed, and there came a flower.
Holy is God, and the world His flower.

THERE was a poor man who had a field, wherein he laboured all day. He had a daughter, an only child, and he loved her. At sunset, after his work, he looked at the field; and twilight fell upon him looking, and the stars came out. God's flower hung over him open, and he knew it not. But he called his daughter from the house, and laid his hand on her head. And he said, " The field bears well: I will buy thee shoes and stockings." So. she made merry in the darkness; and he saw God in her.

At dawn there came an army out of the East, and laid waste the field. They set fire to the house and the goods, and, used the daughter foully. Anger strengthened the man against his enemies, and he killed three of them.

But the rest struck open his head, and threw him away. When they had done, they went; and the girl died.

The man lay all day, knowing nothing. But in the evening he looked up, and saw the sky. And a bright star comforted him with peace; so that he cared not for his pain, thinking of God only. But when he turned a little he saw the girl, and remembered. He crept to her and kissed her hair. And he made a vow.

Therefore when his wound was healed up, he made haste to be a soldier. He went with his companions to the great war, mindful of his daughter. He rejoiced in killing the enemy every day, till he was drunken with the blood of them.

It happened that he came on one dying, that was an enemy. The enemy said, "Stay with me, I pray thee, while I die." He went up to hint slowly to stay with him, frowning upon him. But the enemy said, "Kneel, I pray thee; hold my hand." He kneeled and took the hand of the enemy, awaiting death. The enemy said, "I have two boys, and my wife loves me." They were silent. And the enemy died.

The man left him for the crows and the ants, but he went away grieving. And his spirit flagged, and he lay down. He saw a host of ants on the ground killing one another; but beside him was a great and old tree, whose leaves were innumerable. The wind stirred all the leaves of the tree, making one great sound. The sound gave peace to the man, and he slept.

He woke in the night, and the stars were innumerable. The murmur of the leaves seemed the song of all the stars. And the earth sang also, and life everywhere; and the armies sang, and the dead sang. And he heard his daughter, leading all. Therefore the man listened until the dawn, and until the sun rose. And he stood up before the sun, and made a vow.

He went to his comrades and said, "Brothers, it is a shame to kill; it were better to die. Let us go over to our brothers, and make peace." But they said, "Wilt thou persuade a million? Nay, we must guard the land." But when they were told to attack, the man would not. An officer saw him, and urged him. But the man said, "Brother, it is a shame to kill; it were better to die." The officer was grieved, and killed him.

***

God sowed a seed: it adventured after beauty.
The Goal of all Souls is the beauty of that flower.

There was a young man of noble blood, who would not kill. An enemy rose up against his people, and all hiss friends became soldiers; but the young man stayed at home grieving, and walked alone in the fields. But the enemy devoured the cattle and the harvest, and slaughtered the people; and the young man had no peace with himself, for he doubted. So he went on to a mountain to question with God. He saw the cornfields and the cottages, and the city far away. And he said, "Though I lose my soul, we must save the people."

So he went down with a heavy heart, and became a soldier. He took men into battle, and men were killed. But after the battle he went aside and threw himself on the ground, and wept for the killed, and for the wounded. He cried, "Oh, God deliver me from killing, for my soul sickens."

But again he went into battle, and the slaughter was great. And when it was done, he stood among the dead thinking. He said, "What is death? What evil is in it? Death is deep sleep, and pain is a dream. Where is life, there is strife; and thence grew the soul. And the goal of all grief is God."

Many time afterwards he took men into battle, forcing himself. He thought of the people and the cause only, and would not see the dead. He did deeds of valour and kindness, and was beloved.

One day when he led his men to attack, a man would not. And he urged the man to attack; but the man said, "Brother, it is a shame to kill; it were better to die."

The officer feared lest others should be corrupted, and the cause lost. So he killed the man: but he grieved.

The officer went into battle, and they gained the victory through him. The enemy were slaughtered in thousands, and driven headlong; and the young man became a great commander, honoured of all soldiers. But he lived for the cause; and he grieved.

It happened on a dark night that they brought in his friend dead. So he went out into the wind and the rain, to think about his friend. The rain beat upon him, and there was no clear sky; yet he remembered the stars, desiring them. There was a great wind that bent down the trees; and the leaves and little branches were tom off, scourging his face. He cried aloud to God, saying, "What wilt thou of me? It is far better to die than to kill."

In the morning they brought him a young man of the enemy, saying that he was a spy. But he looked into the eyes of the young man and found no guile in them. The young man said, " Slayer! My work is to make peace between the peoples. The peoples curse war: they curse thee." But the officer told them to release him, and said to him, "Brother, since it is a shame to kill, it is far better to die." And the officer went outside, and killed himself.

***

God sowed a seed, certain of the flower;
But man must doubt till the bud burst.

There was a young man of intelligence, a skilled iron worker. He quarrelled with his masters, so that they threatened him. But he urged his companions to stand by him, for he said, "the right is with me"; and they stopped work and stood by him. After a month they came to him and said, "We are weary;" but he answered, "The cause is just;" and they departed. After another month they came again and said, "Our wives and our children starve;" but he said, "The cause is just;" and they departed. But after another month they came and said, "We are beaten." He said, "Though ye die, the cause is just." But they went back to their work, deserting him.

The young man wandered from city to city, seeking work and the truth. And it happened one night before dawn that he read deeply in a book; but he grew weary of its wisdom, and opened the window; and he looked up among the roofs and the chimneys, and saw a star. He thought, "The stars are thrown hither and thither for no purpose; men are thrown hither and thither, and there is no God." And he thought, "The stars clash not, but men clash; I will make order in earth as in heaven."

But two great armies came out of the East and the West, and the young man was taken away to be a soldier. But he considered while they took him and said, "All peoples are one: it is foolish to make war: I will not." They were angry with him, but he would not be persuaded. So they took him to work in the mines where they could compel him. He laboured under ground all day, and the darkness entered into his soul. He said,

"The rich contrive war, lest the people should rebel. Perish the rich, robbers and murderers."

The young man escaped from the mines, and went between the peoples making peace. But the enemy seized him as a spy and took him before an officer; and the young man cursed the officer, in the name of the peoples. But the officer set him free, and said, "Brother, since it is a shame to kill, it is far better to die. "Then the officer killed himself, and the young man was glad. But the soldiers wept over their officer like children, because they loved him. The young man was ashamed.

He escaped through both armies into the borders of his own country. And he was perplexed because of the officer, and because of God. Now he sat by the roadside thinking, and looking into the blue sky for God. There came a number of carts, wherein were folk and their goods; and the last cart lagged sorely, for the horse was old. An old man and a girl were in the cart, and the girl drove. The young man went along with the last cart and asked, "Who are all ye?" The girl looked at him, and he saw that she was holy. But she turned her eyes from him and said, "The enemy came upon us." His heart smote him because of them, so that he cried, "Cursed be the enemy." But she said, "Who art thou that cursest ?" He answered, "I am a man of peace." She looked into his eyes, saying, " Art thou so?"

The young man went away perplexed, grieving for the old man and the girl. All day long he thought about her, and at night. And he dreamed that he stood among the stars, ordering their courses, and the officer came to him, penitent because he had led one star astray. Therefore he cursed the officer, and sent him to hell. But the girl rose before him, reproaching him; and she said, "His blood is upon thee, and the blood of my father is upon thee. Thou hast killed them in thy self-righteousness. Thou little soul, who playest at God."

In the morning the young man became a soldier to fight for the people. He was stripped of his pride and became humbler than the humblest. And when winter began he went into battle, and fought gladly.

***

God sowed a seed: slowly buds the flower:
God will pluck when he wills.

There was an old man past work, whose daughter tended him. They sat in the doorway of their house in the evening; and the old man talked about his prime, and the girl sewed. But one came running by the house who cried, "The enemy, the enemy!" The old man rose up in anger and said, "God strike them!" But she led him into the house and made him ready for a journey; and she took the savings from the chest, nine gold pieces, and knotted them in a handkerchief, and hid them on her. Then soldiers of the enemy came in riotously, seeking entertainment, and when they saw the girl, rejoiced over her. But she stood before them and said, "Friends, all that we have is yours, but my father and I are not yours, but God's." They saw that she was holy, and they were ashamed; but they told her to go away thence with her father and. their household goods, for there was to be a battle. So she harnessed the old horse to the cart, and set her father in the cart, and gathered the household goods together, and packed them in the cart. Then she climbed up beside her father and drove away.

Upon the road next day they met a young man who was not a soldier. She knew that he was indeed no coward, but a man of peace. and in her heart she honoured him for it, and remembered him.

They continued on the way five days till they came to the place allotted to them. They were given ground and a wooden hut, and there they dwelt. The girl made the house pleasant for her father, and tilled the ground for vegetables. She hired herself out to labour in the fields, for all the young men were at the war. But they that worked with her looked askance at her; for she said, "Would that all were men of peace."

With winter came great cold and the snow; and the old man sickened toward death. He said, "God punish the enemy, who brought us to this." But she answered, "Alas, they are God's children and He loves them." And she said, "Rememberest thou the young man of peace?" He said, "Though the rivers pour blood into the sea, and the peoples die off like autumn leaves; though all lands be wrecked; yet shall the earth be filled full with men of peace."

He laid his hands on his daughter, blessing her; and he said, "God has need of such as thee, my daughter, my darling." Then he died, and she was alone weeping. She laid him out fairly with clean linen, and sat with the dead till dawn, thinking about death.

On a spring evening as she came home through the fields, the young man stood before her who had said, "I am a man of peace." He said, "Because of thee I became a soldier, for my heart smote me. Because of thee I put off my self-righteousness, and fought gladly. But it happened that I chased a man with steel and he tripped. And my hand would not strike him, because he had tripped. A great horror of killing came over me, so that I fled like one mad. I have done with soldiering for ever, though I die for it. That I might tell thee, I have sought thee very many days." Now the girl wondered at his words; and she began to love him. And they two wandered about among the fields, loath to part; but at last they came into her garden, and stood still among the green things. She said, "See the stars, God's children also. Surely they love, and kill not." But he told her about the stars, that they are great suns and worlds; and she said, "They that dwell in those worlds, what of them?" She lifted up her hands to heaven, greeting those peoples; and she said to them, "Brothers and sisters whom I know not; do ye work and weep and love? Then I love you. Do ye hate and kill and make war? Still I love you." Then were they two silent a while before the majesty of the stars, and the mystery of one another. He said, "I knew not what God might be, till thou didst show me. He is the majesty of all the stars, and he is the soul of one girl."

Men came seeking him who arrested him as a deserter. They said, "Brave men are dying, and thou lurkest with a harlot." The young man broke loose raging, and hurt them. But they overpowered him and killed him, and took away the body.

The girl stood still in the pathway of the garden, among the green things. She lifted up her hands again to the heavens, and to the peoples therein; and she cried to them, "Weep with me, weep with me, ye peoples. They have taken my friend." But she wept not. She stood looking from star to star, amazed at death. A great terror and joy seized her because of the near prescence of her friend.

***

God sowed a seed. It shall not fail,
Though in autumn the leaves wither.

The earth was a battlefield, and the cities heaps of ruins. All men were fighting: there were none to work. The armies were hungry and very tired, and still they fought. Women and children lay dead in the open unburied, yet more babies were born. Pestilences ate the peoples; the earth was foul.

Fiercer and fiercer grew the war, and neither side could conquer. The peoples began to rebel, and confusion grew. Yet in all lands were men of peace, working against war; and women of peace, who would not bear sons for the slaughter. Soldiers began to mingle with the enemy and be friends with them between the battles; yet at a word of command they would go back to kill. Everyone said to himself, "War is Hell; there is no good in it." But to his neighbour he said, "We suffer in a great cause." And so war devoured all things and all evil grew.

There was a woman on a battlefield, tending the wounded. The sun burned them and there was no water.

They began to rave, but nothing could be done. The woman ,vas busy over them, but all the while she thought deeply, wondering that men endured so much for war, but for peace they dared nothing.

Now a great mass of men ran thither, chased by the enemy; who slaughtered them as they ran. The woman stood up against them compassionate, but she could not restrain them. They all swept past her raging, and she was left with the newly fallen. But after a while the enemy returned bringing prisoners. They would have seized her; but a holy anger came over her, so that they dared not. She cried, "Friends, ye all hate war; why must ye fight? Are ye mad, that ye can love and yet kill? Or are ye cowards, that ye dare not throw down your weapons? The whole world wants peace, and the whole world is afraid. See the battlefield, your work! Are ye glad of it? Ye hate it, ye hate it, for ye are men, not wolves. Ye have wives and mothers and sweethearts, and children trust you. How can ye kill under the blue sky in June? Oh, we have all lost sight of God, and so we have no joy. Yet

God is in everyone that loves; he is in everyone's heart. Throw down your weapons, throw them down. Better die than kill. Better die men of peace, than live making war. If ye dare, others will dare, and others and others; and so war must end."

A crowd gathered round her to listen, and each man knew that she spoke the truth;. for in everyone's heart a voice answered her voice, the God in each speaking. A murmur rose from the crowd, so that all knew that all approved. And they began throwing down their weapons; and suddenly all shouted for joy. Then the women urged them to scatter over the country-side to speak for peace. And she said, "Most will be killed, but it is for peace."

Suddenly their enemy attacked them, and they let themselves be overpowered. Most were quickly destroyed, but they died praising peace. The enemy were amazed, and faltered in the killing; and soon they also threw away their weapons, and became men of peace.

All that mixed host spread abroad to persuade men to stop war. Many were martyred, but they died in joy. And the peoples were ready to hear; so the word spread. At last it was agreed that on a certain day all war should cease, and all weapons be gathered together and destroyed. And on that day it was done. Each man took a vow, holding the hand of one that had been an enemy. All the armies marched home, and in their homes was joy.

Then men began to build again what had been destroyed, and to set on foot the great works of peace. Everywhere there was sorrow still, and the misery that war had made; but there was hope. Men began to quarrel and to grasp what was within reach; but a new spirit also dawned. The souls of men had been chastened for the beginning of a new age. It shall be an age of knowing God, and an age of joy.

The woman went back to her village and made a home for herself. She grew green stuff for market, and kept fowls. She went to market every week, carrying a full basket. Her neighbours' children loved her and gave her a pet name. And often at night she went into the garden to look at the stars, and to ask them about her friend who was dead She named the stars according to her fancy, knowing them so well. She grew to hear the music that is the song of all the stars. And she knew her friend, and he was God. Then in the time when joy had come back into the world, she died.

God sowed a seed, and there came a flower.
Holy is God, and the world His flower.